DATE DUE		
DEC 2 8 2009			
MAY 1 0 2013			

© THE BAKER & TAYLOR CO.

◆ YOUNG ◆
MERLIN

YOUNG
MERLIN

ROBERT D. SAN SOUCI
illustrated by
DANIEL HORNE

Doubleday
New York London Toronto Sydney Auckland

PUBLISHED BY DOUBLEDAY
a division of Bantam Doubleday Dell Publishing Group, Inc.
666 Fifth Avenue, New York, New York 10103

DOUBLEDAY
and the portrayal of an anchor with a dolphin
are trademarks of Doubleday, a division of
Bantam Doubleday Dell Publishing Group, Inc.

Design by Diane Stevenson/SNAP•HAUS GRAPHICS

Library of Congress Cataloging-in-Publication Data
San Souci, Robert D.
Young Merlin.
Summary: Presents the life of Merlin the magician
from his miraculous birth through the age of seventeen,
before he met King Arthur.
1. Merlin (Legendary character)   [1. Merlin (Legendary
character)   2. Folklore—
England]   I. Horne, Daniel, ill.   II. Title.
PZ8.1.S227Yo 1990 398.2'1'0942   88-30916
ISBN 0-385-24800-8
ISBN 0-385-24801-6 (lib. bdg.)
RL: 3.7

For Michael and Virginia San Souci,
Mark, Michelle, Nicholas, and Robert George
–R.S.S.

◆

To my wife, Joy
–D.H.

There are many stories of
Merlin the Magician's birth,
childhood, and youth.
This is one. . . .

he handsome young man arrived in the village of Carmarthen one misty evening, having come on foot from the distant wood. His green eyes were flecked with gold, and he always had a gold coin in his hand when he needed it.

Not long thereafter, the prettiest young woman in the village fell deeply in love with him, and he took her to be his wife. When she told him they were going to be blessed with a child, he seemed neither pleased nor displeased. But his wife was troubled to find him often staring across the meadows to the distant woods, or standing with his head cocked to one side, as if he were listening to sounds only he could hear.

Just before the child was born, the stranger disappeared into the mists of evening, as mysteriously as he had come. While his wife grieved after him, the villagers whispered that the one who had vanished had surely been an elf or demon. They were sure that his wife was wasting away under some wicked enchantment.

In time, the local priest heard the rumor, and came to sprinkle the woman with holy water, and gave her into the keeping of the good nuns at the nearby convent. This was done for the sake of her soul, and for the soul of her unborn child.

"Holy water or none," the villagers told one another, "no mortal baby will come of *that* union."

But when the child was born, he seemed human enough—though he had a shock of coal-black hair, large ears, and eyes that sometimes seemed to flash with light.

He was named Merlin, and he was a fey little boy, who laughed a great deal but never cried.

The sisters taught him to read and write, and he was a clever child, wise beyond his years—but often disobedient. He would not sit still in chapel—"It makes me itch," he said—and hid when he was called to prayer. His small size made it easy for him to slip away and find a secret hiding place.

But while his mischief vexed the nuns, his strange talents made them fearful. He could see things that were hidden from view, read the future for other people (but not his own fate), and look into the past. Sometimes he said that he could see spirits that haunted lonely roads or woodland shadows.

He loved his mother deeply. He loved to curl up in her lap while she sat by a window or on a garden bench, her eyes filled with secret dreams and her head turned a little to one side, as though she were listening to distant music only she could hear.

At such times, she would tell him that his father was a spirit of air and darkness, a visitor from a shadowy fairyland who appeared to her as a handsome stranger with gold-flecked eyes. She would stroke his unruly black hair, and he would fall asleep, dreaming magical dreams.

When she caught a fever, and the sisters sorrowfully told Merlin his mother was dying, the boy stayed day and night by her side, ready to battle the angel of death. One night, however, he fell asleep and dreamed that death had come into the room. But he had come as a knight in golden armor, and Merlin's mother had risen from her bed and run happily to take his outstretched hand.

The next morning, when he awoke, Mother Hild, the abbess, hugged him and whispered, "You're an orphan now, my child— though a child of God is never truly alone."

Her words gave small comfort to the weeping boy.

Mother Hild told him the sisters would raise him as a ward of the Church. But Merlin soon made her regret this kindness. As he grew older, he tested the nuns' patience by stealing food from the kitchen, asking questions the sisters could not answer, continually being found where he shouldn't be, and never coming when called to run an errand. Mother Hild would grab him by the ear and try to shake some goodness into him, but the boy would slip away with a merry laugh that disturbed the holy silence of the convent.

"Surely there is some elf blood in him," the priest told the sisters. "But he never uses his gifts for wickedness, so we must not call them evil."

The villagers were not so kind. "Devil's child!" they would yell when Merlin went to fetch bread or milk for the sisters. Sometimes the cruelest would throw stones at the boy—only to be routed when the stones turned around in mid-flight and pelted the throwers.

But while this saved the boy some bruises, it did nothing to make him more popular with the villagers.

Often he would hide in the nearby woods. There he would eat nuts and berries and make up wildwood songs that charmed the deer and rabbits to his side. He tamed a huge stag with five-branched horns and a white forefoot and rode him through the forest glades.

Or he would return to the neighboring village, where he heard the folk talk about Vortigern, the King of Britain. He was a wicked man, they said, who had killed the rightful King and had driven the ruler's two sons across the sea to France.

"The princes will soon return," people muttered. "Even now the King is building a great tower to defend himself."

Such news interested Merlin. But when he asked the grown folk about the slain King and far-off princes, they chased him away, saying, "These matters don't concern children. Run off and play."

The village children called him an elf child, because of the stories that his father had come from fairyland. Since he was small for his age, the local bullies would pick fights all the time. But Merlin was tough and had such a temper that he always gave a good accounting of himself in a fight.

One day, when he was playing ball with several of the youngest children, who loved him in spite of their parents' disapproval, the miller's son began to call him names. Though the other boy far outweighed him, Merlin quickly bloodied the bigger boy's nose. Then the bully shouted, "You don't fight fair, you elf child. Your father wasn't human. You've bewitched me!"

Merlin raised his arm to strike again, but his hand was caught in a leather-gloved fist. Looking up, he found that the fist belonged to a mounted knight, whose other hand held the reins of his horse. Several more knights on horseback watched. Their helmets and breastplates were dusty, and their horses' flanks were sweaty, as though they had ridden a great distance.

"Say again what you said about this boy," Merlin's captor ordered the miller's son.

"He's an orphan, the devil's own child," said the boy, wiping his bloody nose. "His mother was human, but his father was a demon."

"You liar!" yelled Merlin, trying to break free. The miller's son stepped back, until he was sure Merlin couldn't twist loose.

"It's true enough," said other villagers, who were standing around gawking.

"King Vortigern ordered us to search the realm until we found a child who had a human mother but no human father," said the soldier. "He must be the one we seek."

He hauled Merlin up and sat the child in front of him on his horse. Then the knights galloped away toward the west.

"Where are you taking me?" Merlin cried.

"To the King," said the soldier, and he refused to answer any other questions the boy put to him.

**S**everal times on their long journey, Merlin tried to escape. But each time he was caught and beaten for his efforts.

Once Merlin asked a farmer sitting beside the road for some water, but the man refused him. Then the boy laughed.

"Why are you laughing?" asked the soldier seated behind him.

"Because that greedy man, who refuses to give away a drop of water, is sitting over a buried treasure."

"How do you know this?"

"Pictures pass before my mind of things that are or will be," said Merlin.

The soldier snorted, clearly not believing a word.

Farther on, they saw a peddler sitting in the shade of a tree. He was eating a loaf of bread and mending an old pair of shoes. When the boy begged a few crumbs, the man ignored him.

Merlin laughed again.

"Why are you laughing?" asked the knight.

"Because the fellow thinks he's going to wear those shoes, but they'll be stolen before he puts them on."

"Faugh!" said the soldier. "A child can't have such powers!"

Next they met a funeral procession. "If you're able to see things," the knight challenged Merlin, "tell me how this man died."

"By falling, by hanging, and by drowning," said the boy.

"How can a man die three deaths?" the soldier sneered.

But an old woman in the procession said, "Indeed, the boy is right. Poor William fell from a rock into a tree, and hung upside down by his heels with his head underwater, and so he drowned."

The soldier was silent, but Merlin knew the man now believed what he said.

At last, they came to Vortigern. The King stood under an awning in front of his fine tent at the foot of a hill, which overlooked the surrounding plain. At its crown, hod carriers, stonemasons, joiners, and other laborers were raising a huge fortress-tower.

Beside the King, arguing among themselves, were three old men with long gray beards and brown robes.

Merlin was dragged before the King. When he protested this rough treatment, the knight, who held him by the tunic, boxed his ears. The boy decided it was better to keep still.

The soldier quickly explained that Merlin was the child they had been sent to find. At this, Vortigern smiled in a way that made Merlin think of a fox just come upon an unguarded henhouse.

"You have been chosen for a great honor, boy," said the King. He pointed toward the half-built fortress at the top of the hill. "Three times I've raised my tower up, and three times it has come crashing down. But my wizards have found the answer."

He beckoned to the old men, who stopped arguing and drew close. The one with the longest beard said, "We have studied the stars carefully. They have told us what Vortigern must do."

The second wizard continued, "Find a boy who had no human father, slay him, and sprinkle his blood on the cornerstone."

The third said, "Then the spirits of this place will let the King's tower stand for a thousand years."

Angrily Merlin shouted, "That is not true! My blood won't help!"

"Quiet!" ordered the King.

"My lord," said the soldier who held Merlin captive, "listen to the lad. He sees what others cannot."

Vortigern looked doubtful, but he said, "Tell me what makes my tower tumble down, and I may spare your life."

So Merlin said, "There are two dragons in a cave beneath your tower. One is white as milk; the other is red as fire. They fight all the time, and their struggle shakes the hill and knocks your tower down."

The wizards called Merlin a liar, but Vortigern silenced them. Then he ordered his laborers to dig into the side of the hill.

They soon broke through into a secret cave, releasing two dragons—red and white, just as Merlin had said—which burst half-blinded into the daylight, hissing and coiling around each other. They scorched each other's scales with blasts of fire.

Merlin and the others ran for cover as the tail of the white dragon flattened Vortigern's tent.

The creatures raged back and forth across the plain, fighting with fang, claw, tail, and flame, until the white one burned the red one to ashes. Then the victor rose into the air and flew slowly away to the west.

After that, Vortigern's tower went up quickly—and remained standing. The King kept Merlin at his court as chief counselor, though the other wizards grumbled about having a child set over them.

But shortly after Vortigern's tower was completed, word came that the sons of the true King—the princes Aurelius and Uther—had come across the sea from France. They were leading a great army against Vortigern.

Vortigern summoned Merlin to his throne room, where he sat surrounded by his nobles and knights.

"Who will win?" the King asked the boy.

"The princes," Merlin answered honestly. "They are like the white dragon. You will die by fire, just as the red dragon did."

"Treason!" screamed Vortigern. "Guards! Seize the traitor and lock him in the deepest dungeon."

But Merlin escaped them as easily as he had once run away

from Mother Hild when she'd caught him stealing bread and honey from the convent kitchen.

He hid behind a curtain until the hue and cry had quieted down. At evening, he slipped out the gates and hurried toward the distant hills that circled the plain. He spent the night in a cave.

In the morning, he awoke to discover the army of the princes camped on the plain below Vortigern's tower. Even as he watched, Vortigern sent his soldiers out to battle. But the King's men surrendered and cast their lot with the princes. Then they laid siege to the tower, setting it afire. Just as Merlin had seen, Vortigern perished in the flames, and his fortress was reduced to ashes.

For a time, Merlin lived happily in the woods, growing into a young man. He learned to unlock the healing magic of plants. He read signs and wonders in cloud shapes or flights of birds or the stars. And he discovered how to change his shape, so that he could take on the form of any man or beast.

Eventually, word of his magic reached the new King, Aurelius, and his brother, Uther, who was general of his army. They decided to invite Merlin to their court, and so they sent a messenger to the magic spring, deep in the forest, where Merlin was most often found.

But Merlin, who loved to joke, turned himself into a huge stag with five-branched horns and a white forefoot. When the King's messenger arrived, he found only the beast drinking at the spring beneath a spreading oak. So he returned empty-handed.

Aurelius sent another messenger, who found an ugly old woman in rags, dipping water out of the spring and pouring it on the roots of a sweet-apple tree. The hag only laughed when asked about Merlin, and so the messenger went away.

Finally Uther went himself and found himself standing across the spring from a ferocious wild man, beside a flowering white thorn. The monster was eighteen feet tall, covered with black, bristly hair, and clad in a wolfskin. He had ears as large as fans, burning eyes as big as an ox's, and a mouth as broad as a dragon's, filled with sharp teeth.

The creature roared and pranced and shook its oaken club at Uther, but the man drew his sword and stood his ground.

Suddenly the wild man began to laugh. Then he called out, "You're a brave one!" Before Uther's eyes, the monster turned into a handsome young man dressed in fine clothes.

"Are you Merlin, who is called the Magician?" asked Uther.

"Indeed," said Merlin, smiling and bowing.

So it was that Merlin entered the service of King Aurelius.

These were dangerous times. Aurelius was a good man and a just King, who ruled wisely and well, but his kingdom was torn apart as first one and then another rebel lord challenged his right to the crown.

Merlin offered wise advice to the King and his brother and helped them with his magic arts. Sometimes, when the King was sorely worried, the young magician would amuse Aurelius and Uther by turning himself into a mischievous dwarf or a beautiful woman or a greyhound or a stag. He became like a third brother to the others; they became the family he had never known.

When reports came that the rebels had combined their armies on Salisbury Plain, Merlin rode beside Aurelius and Uther to meet the enemy. All three knew that the outcome of the struggle would decide the fate of Britain.

The evening before the final battle, Aurelius and Uther came to Merlin's tent, where he sat gazing into the flames in a bronze bowl.

"Will we win tomorrow?" asked Aurelius.

"Yes," said Merlin. But both brothers could see that he was deeply troubled.

"Will my brother and I be safe?" asked Uther.

There were tears in Merlin's eyes as he said, "One of you will die."

After a silence, Aurelius asked, "Which?"

"That I cannot tell you," Merlin said, though he had seen clearly enough who would fall.

he fighting the next day was fierce. Merlin took the form of the giant wild man and spread terror among the enemy. By day's end, the rebels retreated, with the King's army in pursuit.

But Merlin found Aurelius where he knew he would, fallen beneath his battle flag with the picture of a fire-spitting dragon. Tenderly he carried his friend's body back to camp.

At Merlin's urging, Uther was proclaimed King by all the soldiers. And the new King's first command to Merlin was "Raise a fitting monument to my brother here, upon this battlefield. Build him a tomb that will last forever."

Then Merlin had a vision of a circle of standing stones, called the Dance of Giants, on a mountain in Ireland.

Summoning all his magic, he floated the massive bluestones through the night sky and drew them down into a towering circle, just as they had stood in distant Ireland.

At that instant, a huge star of dazzling brightness appeared over the circle of stones. It grew until it became a ball of fire, which took the shape of a dragon. From its mouth blazed rays that extended east and west, as far as the eye could see. Everyone stared and murmured and wondered.

"What does it mean?" asked Uther.

"Take heart," said Merlin, his hand upon his friend's shoulder. "The fiery dragon is you. The rays foretell that you will have a son whose fame will reach to the ends of the earth."

Uther named the circle of standing stones Aurelius's Rest and buried his brother at the center. In the years that followed, however, local folk called it Stonehenge.

And Uther's son was King Arthur, whom Merlin also served, and whose famous legend lives on until today.